◆

The Complete

Tales of Peter Rabbit

And Other Favorite Stories

◆

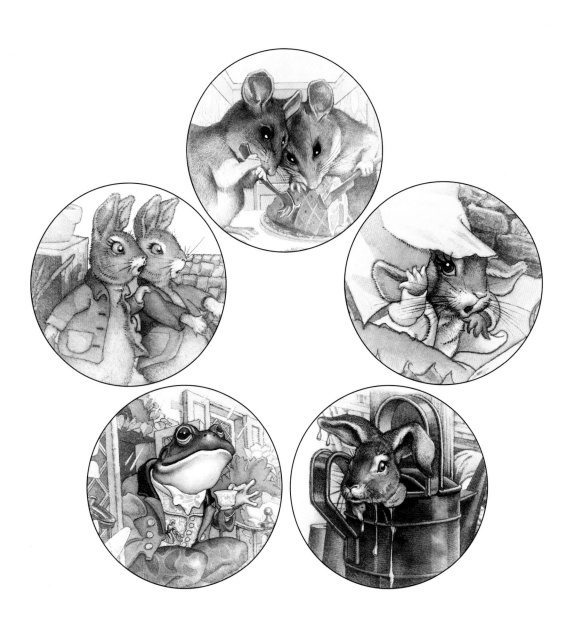

THE COMPLETE
TALES OF PETER RABBIT
AND OTHER FAVORITE STORIES

by Beatrix Potter
Illustrated by Charles Santore

Running Press
Philadelphia ◆ Pennsylvania

Dedications

The dedications to these stories appear as
originally written by Beatrix Potter.

The Tale of Mr. Jeremy Fisher
For Stephanie
From Cousin B.

The Tale of Benjamin Bunny
For the Children of Sawrey
From Old Mr. Bunny

The Tale of Two Bad Mice
For W. M. L. W.
The Little Girl Who Had the Doll's House

The Flopsy Bunnies
For All Little Friends of
Mr. McGregor & Peter & Benjamin

Charles Santore dedicates the illustrations in this book
to his children, Christina, Charlie and Nicholas

Copyright © 1986, 1990 by Running Press
Illustrations copyright © 1986, 1990 by Charles Santore

Canadian representatives: General Publishing Co., Ltd., 30 Lesmill Road,
Don Mills, Ontario M3B 2T6.

9 8 7 6 5 4 3 2 1
The digit on the right indicates the number of this printing.

Library of Congress Cataloging-in-Publication Number
90-52736

ISBN 0-89471-855-X.

Jacket design by Toby Schmidt
Typography by Commcor Communications, Philadelphia,
Pennsylvania and Composing Room, Philadelphia, Pennsylvania.
Printed and bound in Hong Kong by
South Sea International Press, Ltd.

This book may be ordered by mail from the publisher.
Please add $2.50 for postage and handling.
But try your bookstore first!

Running Press Book Publishers
125 South Twenty-second Street, Philadelphia, Pennsylvania 19103

Contents

THE TALE OF PETER RABBIT

Once upon a time
there were four little Rabbits,
and their names were—
Flopsy, Mopsy, Cotton-tail, and Peter.

They lived with their mother in a sand-bank,
underneath the root of a very big fir-tree.

"Now, my dears," said old Mrs. Rabbit one morning, "you may go into the fields or down the lane, but don't go into Mr. McGregor's garden: your father had an accident there; he was put in a pie by Mrs. McGregor."

Then old Mrs. Rabbit took a basket and her umbrella, and went through the wood to the baker's. She bought a loaf of brown bread and five currant buns.

Flopsy, Mopsy, and Cotton-tail, who were good little bunnies, went down the lane to gather blackberries: but Peter, who was very naughty, ran straight away to Mr. McGregor's garden, and squeezed under the gate!

First he ate some lettuces and some French beans; and then he ate some radishes; but round the end of a cucumber frame, whom should he meet but Mr. McGregor!

Mr. McGregor was on his hands and

knees planting out young cabbages, but he jumped up and ran after Peter, waving a rake and calling out, "Stop thief!"

Peter was most dreadfully frightened; he rushed all over the garden, for he had forgotten the way back to the gate.

He lost one of his shoes among the cabbages, and the other shoe amongst the potatoes.

After losing them, he ran on four legs and went faster, so that I think he might have got away altogether if he had not unfortunately run into a gooseberry net, and got caught by the large buttons on his jacket. It was a blue jacket with brass buttons, quite new.

Peter gave himself up for lost, and shed big tears; but his sobs were overheard by some friendly sparrows, who flew to him in great excitement, and implored him to exert himself.

9

Mr. McGregor came up with a sieve, which he intended to pop upon the top of Peter; but Peter wriggled out just in time, leaving his jacket behind him, and rushed into the tool-shed, and jumped into a can. It would have been a beautiful thing to hide in, if it had not had so much water in it.

Mr. McGregor was quite sure that Peter was somewhere in the tool-shed, perhaps hidden underneath a flower-pot. He began to turn them over carefully, looking under each.

Presently Peter sneezed—"Kertyschoo!" Mr. McGregor was after him in no time, and tried to put his foot upon Peter, who jumped out of a window, upsetting three plants. The window was too small for Mr. McGregor, and he was tired of running after Peter. He went back to his work.

Peter sat down to rest; he was out of breath and trembling with fright, and he had not the least idea which way to go. Also he was very damp with sitting in that can.

After a time he began to

wander about, going lippity—lippity—not very fast, and looking all around.

He found a door in a wall; but it was locked, and there was no room for a fat little rabbit to squeeze underneath.

An old mouse was running in and out over the stone doorstep, carrying peas and beans to her family in the wood. Peter asked her the way to the gate, but she had such a large pea in her mouth that she could not answer. She only shook her head at him. Peter began to cry.

Then he tried to find his way straight across

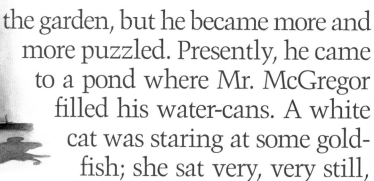

the garden, but he became more and more puzzled. Presently, he came to a pond where Mr. McGregor filled his water-cans. A white cat was staring at some gold-fish; she sat very, very still, but now and then the tip of her tail twitched as if it were alive. Peter thought it best to go away without speaking to her; he had heard about cats from his cousin, little Benjamin Bunny.

He went back towards the tool-shed, but suddenly, quite close to him, he heard the noise of a hoe—scr-r-ritch, scratch, scratch, scritch. Peter scuttered underneath the bushes. But presently, as nothing happened, he came out, and climbed upon a wheelbarrow and peeped over. The first thing he saw was Mr. McGregor hoeing onions. His back was turned towards Peter, and beyond him was the gate!

Peter got down very quietly off the wheelbarrow, and started running as fast as he could go, along a straight walk behind some black-currant bushes.

Mr. McGregor caught sight of him at the corner, but Peter did not care. He slipped underneath the gate, and was safe at last in the wood

outside the garden.

Mr. McGregor hung up the little jacket and the shoes for a scarecrow to frighten the blackbirds.

Peter never stopped running or looked behind him till he got home to the big fir-tree.

He was so tired that he flopped down upon the nice soft sand on the floor of the rabbit-hole and shut his eyes. His mother was busy cooking; she wondered what he had done with his clothes.

It was the second little jacket and pair of shoes that Peter had lost in a fortnight!

I am sorry to say that Peter was not very well during the evening.

His mother put him to bed, and made some camomile tea; and she gave a dose of it to Peter!

"One tablespoonful to be taken at bedtime."

But Flopsy, Mopsy, and Cotton-tail had bread and milk and blackberries for supper.

THE TALE OF MR. JEREMY FISHER

Once upon a time
there was a frog called
Mr. Jeremy Fisher;

he lived in a little damp house amongst the
buttercups at the edge of a pond.
  The water was all slippy-sloppy in the
larder and in the back passage.

But Mr. Jeremy liked getting his feet wet; nobody ever scolded him, and he never caught a cold!

He was quite pleased when he looked out and saw large drops of rain, splashing in the pond—

"I will get some worms and go fishing and catch a dish of minnows for my dinner," said Mr. Jeremy Fisher. "If I catch more than five fish, I will invite my friends Mr. Alderman Ptolemy Tortoise and Sir Isaac Newton. The Alderman, however, eats salad."

Mr. Jeremy put on a macintosh, and a pair of shiny goloshes; he took his rod and basket, and set off with enormous hops to the place where he kept his boat.

The boat was round and green, and very like the other lily-leaves. It was tied to a water-plant in the middle of the pond.

Mr. Jeremy took a reed pole, and pushed the boat out into open water. "I know a good place for minnows," said Mr. Jeremy Fisher.

Mr. Jeremy stuck his pole into the mud and fastened his boat to it.

Then he settled himself cross-legged and

arranged his fishing tackle. He had the dearest little red float. His rod was a tough stalk of grass, his line was a fine long white horse-hair, and he tied a little wriggling worm at the end.

The rain trickled down his back, and for nearly an hour he stared at the float.

"This is getting tiresome; I think I should like some lunch," said Mr. Jeremy Fisher.

He punted back again amongst the water-plants, and took some lunch out of his basket.

"I will eat a butterfly sandwich, and wait till the shower is over," said Mr. Jeremy Fisher.

A great big water-beetle came up underneath the lily leaf and tweaked the toe of one of his goloshes.

Mr. Jeremy crossed his legs up shorter, out of reach, and went on eating his sandwich.

Once or twice something moved about with a rustle and a splash amongst the rushes at the side of the pond.

17

"I trust that is not a rat," said Mr. Jeremy Fisher; "I think I had better get away from here." Mr. Jeremy shoved the boat out again a little way, and dropped in the bait. There was a bite almost directly; the float gave a tremendous bobbit!

"A minnow! a minnow! I have him by the nose!" cried Mr. Jeremy Fisher, jerking up his rod.

But what a horrible surprise! Instead of a smooth fat minnow, Mr. Jeremy landed little Jack Sharp the stickleback, covered with spines!

The stickleback floundered about the boat, pricking and snapping until he was quite out of breath. Then he jumped back into the water.

And a shoal of other little fishes put their heads out, and laughed at Mr. Jeremy Fisher.

And while Mr. Jeremy sat disconsolately on

the edge of his boat—sucking his sore fingers and peering down into the water—a *much* worse thing happened; a really *frightful* thing it would have been, if Mr. Jeremy had not been wearing a macintosh!

A great big enormous trout came up—ker-pflop-p-p-p! with a splash—and it seized Mr. Jeremy with a snap, "Ow! Ow! Ow!"—and dived down to the bottom of the pond!

But the trout was so displeased with the taste of the macintosh, that in less than half a minute it spat him out again; and the only thing it swallowed was Mr. Jeremy's goloshes.

Mr. Jeremy bounced up to the surface of the water, like a cork and the bubbles out of a soda water bottle; and he swam with all his might to the edge of the pond.

He scrambled out on the first bank he came to, and he hopped home across the meadow with his macintosh all in tatters.

"What a mercy that was not a pike!" said
Mr. Jeremy Fisher. "I have lost my rod and basket;
but it does not much matter, for I am sure I
should never have dared to go fishing again!"

He put some sticking plaster on his fingers,
and his friends both came to dinner. He could
not offer them fish, but he had something else
in his larder.

Sir Isaac Newton wore his black and gold
waistcoat, and Mr. Alderman Ptolemy Tortoise

brought a salad with him in a string bag.

And instead of a nice dish of minnows—they had a roasted grasshopper with lady-bird sauce, which frogs consider a beautiful treat; but *I* think it must have been nasty!

22

THE TALE OF BENJAMIN BUNNY

One morning
a little rabbit sat on a bank.

He pricked his ears and listened to the trit-trot,
trit-trot of a pony.

A gig was coming along the road; it was
driven by Mr. McGregor, and beside him sat
Mrs. McGregor in her best bonnet.

As soon as they had passed, little Benjamin Bunny slid down into the road, and set off—with a hop, skip and a jump—to call upon his relations, who lived in the wood at the back of Mr. McGregor's garden.

That wood was full of rabbit holes; and in the neatest sandiest hole of all, lived Benjamin's aunt and his cousins—Flopsy, Mopsy, Cotton-tail and Peter.

Old Mrs. Rabbit was a widow; she earned her living by knitting rabbit-wool mittens and muffetees (I once bought a pair at a bazaar). She also sold herbs, and rosemary tea, and rabbit-tobacco (which is what *we* call lavender).

Little Benjamin did not very much want to see his aunt.

He came round the back of the fir-tree, and nearly tumbled upon the top of his cousin Peter.

Peter was sitting by himself. He looked poorly, and was dressed in a red cotton pocket-handkerchief.

"Peter,"—said little Benjamin, in a whisper—"who has got your clothes?"

Peter replied—"The scarecrow in Mr. McGregor's garden," and described how he had been chased about the garden, and had dropped

his shoes and coat.

Little Benjamin sat down beside his cousin, and assured him that Mr. McGregor had gone out in a gig, and Mrs. McGregor also; and certainly for the day, because she was wearing her best bonnet.

Peter said he hoped that it would rain.

At this point, old Mrs. Rabbit's voice was heard inside the rabbit hole, calling—"Cotton-tail! Cotton-tail! fetch some more camomile!"

Peter said he thought he might feel

better if he went for a walk.

They went away hand in hand, and got upon the flat top of the wall at the bottom of the wood. From here they looked down into Mr. McGregor's garden. Peter's coat and shoes were plainly to be seen upon the scarecrow, topped with an old tam-o-shanter of Mr. McGregor's.

Little Benjamin said, "It spoils people's clothes to squeeze under a gate; the proper way to get in, is to climb down a pear tree."

Peter fell down head first; but it was of no consequence, as the bed below was newly raked and quite soft.

It had been sown with lettuces.

They left a great many odd little footmarks

all over the bed, especially little Benjamin, who was wearing clogs.

Little Benjamin said that the first thing to be done was to get back Peter's clothes, in order that they might be able to use the pocket-handkerchief.

They took them off the scarecrow. There had been rain during the night; there was water in the shoes, and the coat was somewhat shrunk.

Benjamin tried on the tam-o-shanter, but it was too big for him.

Then he suggested that they should fill the pocket-handkerchief with onions, as a little present for his aunt.

Peter did not seem to be enjoying himself; he kept hearing noises.

Benjamin, on the contrary, was perfectly at home, and ate a lettuce leaf. He said that he was in the habit of coming to the garden with his father to get lettuces for their Sunday dinner.

(The name of little Benjamin's papa was old Mr. Benjamin Bunny.)

The lettuces certainly were very fine.

Peter did not eat anything; he said he should like to go home. Presently he dropped half the onions.

Little Benjamin said that it was not possible

to get back up the pear tree, with a load of vegetables. He led the way boldly towards the other end of the garden. They went along a little walk on planks, under a sunny red-brick wall.

The mice sat on their doorsteps cracking cherry-stones; they winked at Peter Rabbit and little Benjamin Bunny.

Presently Peter let the pocket-handkerchief go again.

They got amongst flower-pots, and frames and tubs. Peter heard noises worse than ever;

his eyes were as big
as lolly-pops!

He was a step or two
in front of his cousin, when
he suddenly stopped.

This is what those little
rabbits saw round that corner!

Little Benjamin took one look,
and then, in half a minute less than
no time, he hid himself and Peter
and the onions underneath a
large basket. . . .

The cat got up and stretched
herself, and came and sniffed at
the basket. Perhaps she liked the
smell of onions!

Anyway, she sat down upon the top
of the basket.

♦♦♦

She sat there for *five hours.*

♦♦♦

I cannot draw you a picture of Peter and Benjamin underneath the basket, because it was quite dark, and because the smell of onions was fearful; it made Peter Rabbit and little Benjamin cry.

The sun got round behind the wood, and it was quite late in the afternoon; but still the cat sat upon the basket.

At length there was a pitter-patter, pitter-patter, and some bits of mortar fell from the wall above.

The cat looked up and saw old Mr. Benjamin Bunny prancing along the top of the wall of the upper terrace.

He was smoking a pipe of rabbit-tobacco, and had a little switch in his hand.

He was looking for his son.

Old Mr. Bunny had no opinion whatever of cats.

He took a tremendous jump off the top of the wall on to the top of the cat, and cuffed it off the basket, and kicked it into the green-house, scratching off a handful of fur.

The cat was too much surprised to scratch back.

When old Mr. Bunny had driven the cat into the green-house, he locked the door.

Then he came back to the basket and took

out his son Benjamin by the ears, and whipped him with the little switch.

Then he took out his nephew Peter.

Then he took out the handkerchief of onions, and marched out of the garden.

When Mr. McGregor returned about half an hour later, he observed several things which perplexed him.

It looked as though some person had been walking all over the garden in a pair of clogs—only the footmarks were too ridiculously little!

Also he could not understand how the cat could have managed to shut herself up *inside* the greenhouse, locking the door upon the *outside*.

When Peter got home, his mother forgave him, because she was so glad to see that he had found his shoes and coat. Cotton-tail and Peter folded up the pocket-handkerchief, and old Mrs. Rabbit strung up the onions and hung them from the kitchen ceiling, with the bunches of herbs and the rabbit-tobacco.

THE TALE OF TWO BAD MICE

Once upon a time
there was a very beautiful doll's-house;

it was red brick with white windows, and it had real muslin curtains and a front door and a chimney.

It belonged to two Dolls called Lucinda and Jane; at least it belonged to Lucinda, but she never ordered meals.

Jane was the Cook; but she never did any cooking, because the dinner had been bought ready-made, in a box full of shavings.

There were two red lobsters and a ham, a fish, a pudding, and some pears and oranges.

They would not come off the plates, but they were extremely beautiful.

One morning Lucinda and Jane had gone out for a drive in the doll's perambulator. There was no one in the nursery, and it was very quiet. Presently there was a little scuffling, scratching noise in a corner near the fire-place, where there was a hole under the skirting-board.

Tom Thumb put out his head for a moment, and then popped it in again.

Tom Thumb was a mouse.

A minute afterwards, Hunca Munca, his wife, put her head out, too; and when she saw that there was no one in the nursery, she ventured out on the oilcloth under the coal-box.

The doll's house stood

at the other side of the fire-place. Tom Thumb and Hunca Munca went cautiously across the hearth-rug. They pushed the front door—it was not fast.

Tom Thumb
and Hunca Munca
went upstairs and
peeped into the din-
ing-room. Then they
squeaked with joy!
Such a lovely din-
ner was laid out
upon the table!
There were
tin spoons, and lead
knives and forks,
and two dolly chairs
—all *so* convenient!
Tom Thumb
set to work at once
to carve the ham.
It was a beautiful
shiny yellow,
streaked with red.
The knife crumpled
up and hurt him;
he put his finger
in his mouth.

"It is not boiled enough; it is hard. You have
a try, Hunca Munca."

Hunca Munca stood up in her chair, and chopped at the ham with another lead knife. "It's as hard as the hams at the cheese-monger's," said Hunca Munca. The ham broke off the plate with a jerk, and rolled under the table. "Let it alone," said Tom Thumb; "give me some fish, Hunca Munca!" Hunca Munca tried every tin spoon in turn; the fish was glued to the dish. Then Tom Thumb lost his temper. He put the ham in the middle of the floor, and hit it with the tongs and with the shovel—bang, bang, smash, smash!

The ham flew all into pieces, for underneath the shiny paint it was made of nothing but plaster!

Then there was no end to the rage and disappointment of Tom Thumb and Hunca Munca. They broke up the pudding, the lobsters, the pears and the oranges.

As the fish would not come off the plate, they put it into the red-hot crinkly paper fire in the kitchen; but it would not burn either.

Tom Thumb went up the kitchen chimney and looked out at the top—there was no soot.

While Tom Thumb was up the chimney, Hunca Munca had another disappointment. She found some tiny canisters upon the dresser, labelled— Rice—Coffee—Sago—but when she turned them upside down, there was nothing inside except red and blue beads.

Then those mice set to work to do all the mischief they could—especially Tom Thumb! He took Jane's clothes out of the chest of drawers in her bedroom, and he threw them out of the top floor window.

But Hunca Munca had a frugal mind. After pulling half the feathers out of Lucinda's bolster, she remembered that she herself was in want of a feather bed.

With Tom Thumb's assistance she carried the bolster downstairs, and across the hearthrug. It

was difficult to squeeze the bolster into the mouse-hole; but they managed it somehow.

Then Hunca Munca went back and fetched a chair, a book-case, a bird-cage, and several small odds and ends. The book-case and the bird-cage refused to go into the mouse-hole.

Hunca Munca left them behind the coal-box,

42

and went to fetch a cradle.

Hunca Munca was just returning with another chair, when suddenly there was a noise of talking outside upon the landing. The mice rushed back to their hole, and the Dolls came into the nursery.

What a sight met the eyes of Jane and Lucinda!

Lucinda sat upon the upset kitchen stove and stared; and Jane leant against the kitchen dresser and smiled—but neither of them made any remark.

The book-case and the bird-cage were rescued from under the coal-box—but Hunca Munca has got the cradle, and some of Lucinda's clothes.

She also has some useful pots and pans, and several other things.

The little girl that the doll's-house belonged to, said "I will get a doll dressed like a policeman!"

But the nurse said—"I will set a mouse-trap!"

So that is the story of the two Bad Mice—but they were not so very very naughty after all, because Tom Thumb paid for everything he broke.

He found a crooked sixpence under the hearth-rug; and upon Christmas Eve, he and Hunca Munca stuffed it into one of the stockings of Lucinda and Jane.

And very early every morning—before anybody is awake—Hunca Munca comes with her dust-pan and her broom to sweep the Dollies' house!

The Tale of the Flopsy Bunnies

It is said that the effect
of eating too much lettuce
is "soporific."

I have never felt sleepy after eating lettuces;
but then *I* am not a rabbit.

They certainly had a very soporific effect
upon the Flopsy Bunnies!

When Benjamin Bunny grew up, he married his Cousin Flopsy. They had a large family, and they were very improvident and cheerful.

I do not remember the separate names of their children; they were generally called the "Flopsy Bunnies."

As there was not always quite enough to eat, Benjamin used to borrow cabbages from Flopsy's brother, Peter Rabbit, who kept a nursery garden.

Sometimes Peter Rabbit had no cabbages to spare.

When this happened, the Flopsy Bunnies went across the field to a rubbish heap, in the ditch outside Mr. McGregor's garden.

Mr. McGregor's rubbish heap was a mixture. There were jam pots and paper bags, and

mountains of chopped grass from the mowing machine (which always tasted oily), and some rotten vegetable marrows and an old boot or two. One day—oh joy!—there were a quantity of over-grown lettuces, which had "shot" into flower.

The Flopsy Bunnies simply stuffed lettuces. By degrees, one after another, they were overcome with slumber, and lay down in the mown grass.

Benjamin was not so much overcome as his children. Before going to sleep he was sufficiently wide awake to put a paper bag over his head to

keep off the flies.

The little Flopsy Bunnies slept delightfully in the warm sun. From the lawn beyond the garden came the distant clacketty sound of the mowing machine. The blue-bottles buzzed about the wall, and a little old mouse picked over the rubbish among the jam pots.

(I can tell you her name, she was called Thomasina Tittlemouse, a woodmouse with a long tail.)

She rustled across the paper bag, and awakened Benjamin Bunny.

The mouse apologized profusely, and said that she knew Peter Rabbit.

While she

and Benjamin were talking, close under the wall, they heard a heavy tread above their heads; and suddenly Mr. McGregor emptied out a sackful of lawn mowings right upon the top of the sleeping Flopsy Bunnies! Benjamin shrank down under his paper bag. The mouse hid in a jam pot.

The little rabbits smiled sweetly in their sleep under the shower of grass; they did not awake because the lettuces had been so soporific.

They dreamt that their mother Flopsy was tucking them up in a hay bed.

Mr. McGregor looked down after emptying his sack. He saw some funny little brown tips of ears sticking up through the lawn mowings. He stared at them for some time.

Presently a fly settled on one of them and it moved.

Mr. McGregor climbed down on to the rubbish heap—

"One, two, three, four! five! six leetle rabbits!" said he as he dropped them into his sack. The Flopsy Bunnies dreamt that their mother was turning them over in bed. They stirred a little in their sleep, but still they did not wake up.

Mr. McGregor tied up the sack and left it on the wall.

He went to put away the mowing machine.

While he was gone, Mrs. Flopsy Bunny (who had remained at home) came across the field.

She looked suspiciously at the sack and wondered where everybody was?

Then the mouse came out of her jam pot, and Benjamin took the paper bag off his head, and they told the doleful tale.

Benjamin and Flopsy were in despair; they could not undo the string.

But Mrs. Tittlemouse was a resourceful person. She nibbled a hole

in the bottom corner of the sack.

The little rabbits were pulled out and pinched to wake them.

Their parents stuffed the empty sack with three rotten vegetable marrows, an old blacking-brush and two decayed turnips.

Then they all hid under a bush and watched for Mr. McGregor.

Mr. McGregor came back and picked up the sack, and carried it off.

He carried it hanging down, as if it were rather heavy.

The Flopsy Bunnies followed at a safe distance.

They watched him go into his house.

And then they crept up to the window to listen.

Mr. McGregor threw down the sack on the stone floor in a way that would have been extremely painful to the Flopsy Bunnies, if they had happened to have been inside it.

They could hear him drag his chair on the flags, and chuckle— "One, two, three, four, five, six leetle rabbits!" said Mr. McGregor.

"Eh? What's that? What have they been

spoiling now?" enquired Mrs. McGregor.

"One, two, three, four, five, six leetle fat rabbits!" repeated Mr. McGregor, counting on his fingers—"one, two, three—"

"Don't you be silly; what do you mean, you silly old man?"

"In the sack! one, two, three, four, five, six!" replied Mr. McGregor.

(The youngest Flopsy Bunny got upon the window-sill.)

Mrs. McGregor took hold of the sack and felt it. She said she could feel six, but they must be *old* rabbits, because they were so hard and all different shapes.

"Not fit to eat; but the skins will do fine to line my old cloak."

"Line your old cloak?" shouted Mr. McGregor—"I shall sell them and buy myself baccy!"

"Rabbit tobacco! I shall skin them and cut off their heads."

Mrs. McGregor untied the sack and put her hand inside.

When she felt the vegetables she became very very angry. She said that Mr. McGregor had "done it a purpose."

And Mr. McGregor was very angry too. One of the rotten marrows came flying through the kitchen window, and hit the youngest Flopsy Bunny.

It was rather hurt.

Then Benjamin and Flopsy thought that it was time to go home.

So Mr. McGregor did not get his tobacco, and Mrs. McGregor did not get her rabbit skins.

But next Christmas Thomasina Tittlemouse got a present of enough rabbit-wool to make herself a cloak and a hood, and a handsome muff and a pair of warm mittens.